Take a Hike

Published by Magination Press in partnership with National Wildlife Federation
maginationpress.org and nwf.org

Distributed by Lerner Publisher Services
lernerbooks.com

Written by Kate Chynoweth
Edited by Katie ten Hagen and Julie Spalding
Book design by Chris Gaugler
Produced by WonderLab Group LLC
Printed by Corporate Graphics, North Mankato, MN

Library of Congress Cataloging-in-Publication Data

Names: Chynoweth, Kate, author.

Title: Take a hike! : and other ways to de-stress and relax in nature / by Kate Chynoweth.

Description: Washington, DC : Magination Press, [2025] | Audience term: Preteens | Audience term: Junior high school students | Summary: "This tween-friendly handbook encourages kids to seek out nature for health benefits and planet protection. Kids who spend more time in nature benefit in mind, body, and spirit! And likewise, benefit the Earth"—Provided by publisher.

Identifiers: LCCN 2024038587 (print) | LCCN 2024038588 (ebook) | ISBN 9781433845208 (hardcover) | ISBN 9781433845215 (paperback) | ISBN 9781433845222 (ebook)

Classification: LCC BF353.5.N37 C468 2025 (print) | LCC BF353.5.N37 (ebook) | DDC 155.91—dc23/eng/20240911

LC record available at https://lccn.loc.gov/2024038587 | LC ebook record available at https://lccn.loc.gov/2024038588

Manufactured in the United States of America
10 9 8 7 6 5 4 3 2 1

Take a Hike

AND OTHER WAYS TO DE-STRESS AND RELAX IN NATURE

Contents

Introduction

This book is all about why being outside matters: how it can help you de-stress and relax—and enrich your life in other ways, too! According to research, more time in nature helps build your creativity, emotional resilience, focus, strength, balance, and improves your mood. Yet today, young people spend less time outside than any generation that has come before, as technology and screens occupy more time than ever.

My hope is that this book will inspire you to change that pattern! Create time in your life for awesome experiences in nature, from hiking a rocky trail to seeing dark night skies full of stars. This will help you engage and bond with nature and its amazing creatures, and creating this connection matters a lot. Why? Because we all care most about things we have good experiences with. If you love exploring the woods as a kid, you grow up caring about trees. If your idea of fun is playing in the surf, you value keeping our oceans healthy. Basically, having these early connections motivates you to care for the planet. That matters deeply at a time when climate change is causing more havoc.

The activities and ideas in this book offer fun, creative, and mindful ways to connect with nature—and yourself—in ways that promote happiness. The more time you spend outside, the more you'll discover joys and adventures you can't have through screens or when you're surrounded by walls. Open the door! Nature is waiting.

—*Kate Chynoweth*

How to Use This Book

Activity sections give you ideas for outdoor pursuits and nature-related crafts that are relaxing and fun.

Natural Wonders sections explain more about some of the amazing natural phenomena that exist on our planet.

Climate Spotlight sections highlight creative solutions and technologies helping combat the negative impacts of climate change.

Science Says sidebars investigate how science can explain or assist with questions about nature.

Make a Mini Habit sidebars offer easy ideas for small, simple actions you can take to have a positive impact on the health of our planet.

Dream Destinations sections offer ideas for places you might go for the outdoor experience of a lifetime. If you won't be traveling soon, many of these destinations offer live cameras where you check out views and wildlife action from the comfort of home.

CHAPTER ONE

Nature All Around

Spending time in nature benefits you in lots of ways, from building your creativity, strength, and balance to simply making you happier. And it's all around us! Even if you live in a busy city or suburb, birds fly through the skies and squirrels scamper in the trees.

This chapter is packed with ideas for activities you can accomplish in easily accessible nature areas, the kind that are usually not too far from your front (or back!) door. Whether you take a walk in your neighborhood or visit a local park, playground, or community garden, there is always fun to be had. As you spend more time outside, you will see for yourself how nature can be a positive force in your daily life.

What's your favorite thing to do outdoors?

If you're short on time, don't forget that little moments count, too, like taking a short walk around the block or eating outdoors when the weather is warm. Put away screens and take notice of what's around you, especially in spring and summer when bright flowers pop up even in tiny sidewalk cracks!

The types of flowers you see will vary depending on the climate where you live. In the north, you might see shasta daisies and lilacs, while heading south you might spot azaleas and orange blossoms. In the west, bright poppies flourish, while in tropical Hawaii, yellow hibiscuses bloom. Some flowers, like black-eyed Susans and sunflowers, are common across all of the United States!

Make a Pressed Flower

For this activity, look for common flowers that grow wild in parks, near playgrounds, or on roadsides, always steering clear of gardens you don't have permission to pick from.

What You'll Need:
  Fresh flowers
  Wax paper, plain tissues, or printer paper
  A heavy book, like a dictionary

Activity:

1. Pick delicate, colorful flowers with thinner stalks, like daisies, pansies, or poppies; these work best for pressing, while thicker flowers such as roses do not (although you can just press the petals, if you like). Select flowers that are not wet.

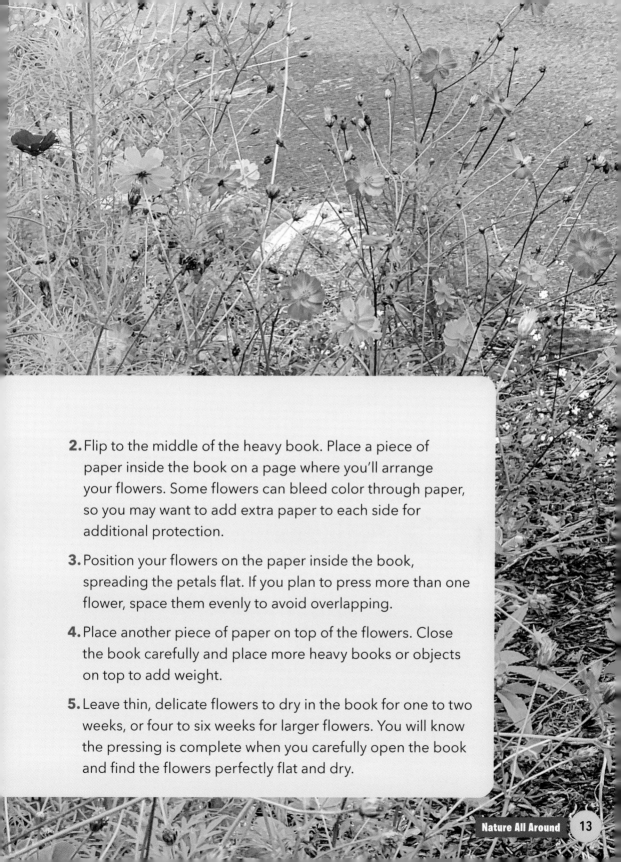

2. Flip to the middle of the heavy book. Place a piece of paper inside the book on a page where you'll arrange your flowers. Some flowers can bleed color through paper, so you may want to add extra paper to each side for additional protection.

3. Position your flowers on the paper inside the book, spreading the petals flat. If you plan to press more than one flower, space them evenly to avoid overlapping.

4. Place another piece of paper on top of the flowers. Close the book carefully and place more heavy books or objects on top to add weight.

5. Leave thin, delicate flowers to dry in the book for one to two weeks, or four to six weeks for larger flowers. You will know the pressing is complete when you carefully open the book and find the flowers perfectly flat and dry.

Green is good for you! Scientists are learning through new studies the positive impacts of being in green space. Some of the interesting findings include:

✳ Views of nature are **restorative**. A view of treetops from a window can help high stress levels drop lower within minutes!

✳ Outdoors can be a space where you get to make your own rules and pursue how to play, on your own schedule. This promotes creativity and **resilience**.

✳ Running, jumping, swinging, climbing: you play harder outdoors than indoors. While you're in the fresh air having fun, you are also building strength, honing balance, and developing other essential physical skills.

FUN FACT

Over 50 billion birds currently live on Earth!

Species Identification With AI

Species identification is a complex science that classifies and names **organisms**. But you don't have to be an expert botanist or trained biologist to identify the many plants and animals around you, thanks to the identification apps available now on smartphones.

These tools are the result of artificial intelligence (AI), which can absorb huge databases of information and images. Since AI data isn't always correct, many apps also rely on engaged users to download their own pictures and identifications to create information that's even more accurate.

This remarkable technology makes it easier than ever to learn fascinating details about other species who share the planet. Even scientists use these apps! For example, some apps provide an effective way to track the arrival of **invasive species**, so that a **conservation** and rescue plan might be put in place. Ask for an adult's help to learn more about one of these apps:

► Merlin Bird ID: identifies bird species; if you have a computer instead of a phone, check out the partner website, All About Birds

► Seek by iNaturalist: identifies animals, fungi, and plants, and has fun chances to earn badges for observation

Rivers and Streams

If you've ever seen a big river—and most big cities are built near or even right on top of one!—you might have wondered: Where does all that water come from, anyway?

Rivers begin as smaller bodies of water called creeks, which travel and grow into streams. When streams merge together, flowing faster and faster down toward sea level, they eventually form a river.

Waterways change with the seasons. If you have rivers, creeks, or streams nearby, make time to quietly **observe** them at different times of year:

Spring: Walk along the edge of a creek or stream to spot frog eggs or tadpoles. Keep an eye out for fluffy goslings and ducklings paddling alongside their mothers.

Summer: Wade into the water to get a closer peek at aquatic plants and creatures, from frogs to lily pads. Or, try fishing if you have the opportunity.

Water Journaling

Spend 20 minutes walking along a shoreline, or in the summer, float on an inner tube, paddle board, canoe, or kayak.

Bring a blank journal and colored pencils. Draw pictures of what you see and note the sounds you hear.

If reaching a water destination is a challenge, check out a fountain in a park that draws birds and squirrels, or visit a botanical garden with water features, like the koi pond traditionally found in Japanese-style gardens.

Create a collection of experiences by bringing the journal when you will be near the water.

Fall: Watch for changing water levels. By autumn, all the snow in the mountains has finished melting and is no longer flowing into streams below.

Winter: Notice how the water habitat changes in cold weather. Does the surface freeze? If you spot fewer animals and birds, look for what they leave behind instead, like tracks, droppings, dens, or dams.

Does your neighborhood
have access to a park with big trees, a waterfront path, or a greenway bike trail? Take note of interesting outdoor places like this (always let an adult know if you're going to visit one)! Or, simply look outside and identify the plants and animals you can see from your window. Nature is all around— and exploring is fun!

Neighborhood Nature Map

In a few short steps you can create a simple map of your neighborhood that highlights nature areas.

What You'll Need:

Graph paper or blank paper

Something to draw with

Ruler

Compass (physical or app)

Measuring tool
(tape measure or app)

Small notebook

Activity:

1. Find north: Use a physical compass or a map app on a smartphone to find the true north direction in your neighborhood.

2. Near the top of the paper, draw a **compass rose** with the north arrow pointing where you found it to be. Add arrows for the other corresponding directions: east, south, and west.

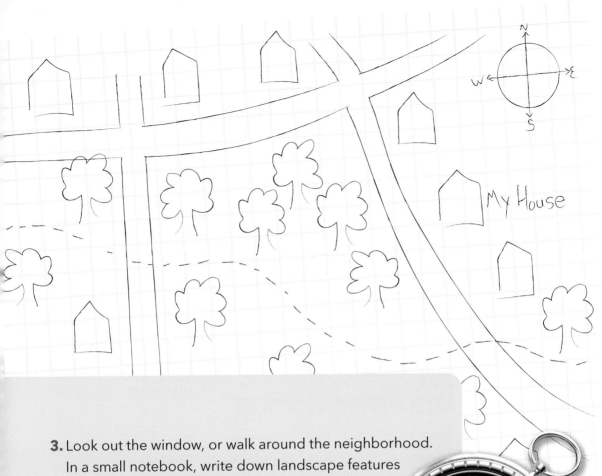

My House

KEY

⌂ = House

🌳 = Tree

- - - - = Path

───── = Street

3. Look out the window, or walk around the neighborhood. In a small notebook, write down landscape features that catch your eye. What size are the houses or buildings, and how many are there? Are there trees? Is it hilly or flat? How much of the sky can you see overhead?

4. Draw and label a square that represents your house or building. Then draw and label your street.

5. Create a map key to add interest to your map. Choose symbols to represent specific features you noticed, like a favorite tree, playgrounds, bright flowers, or areas where squirrels or birds gather. Finally, add and label symbols from your key, and any shapes or other features you noted.

Dark night skies are an essential part of life's rhythms—but you might hardly notice them! That's partly because artificial light is all around you, from the light you switch on in the morning to the bright screens of laptops and phones.

Get extra time away from artificial light and screens, especially in the evenings, and see how it affects you. And always turn off the light before you go to sleep: Research shows even a small amount of light hitting your eyelids shifts you to a more alert state and disrupts your sleep cycle.

Moon and Mood Tracker

The phases of the moon might remind you of your own moods, which change from day to day (sometimes minute to minute). What emotion do you feel when you observe the night sky? Writing down daily observations about the moon, and about your feelings, is an easy practice that can help you feel more in touch with yourself and more at peace.

What You'll Need:

Journal or notebook

Pens or pencils

Colored markers

A moon phase chart

Ruler

Binoculars (if you want more detailed observations)

Activity:

1. Print a moon phase chart from an online source and paste it in your journal, or draw one yourself.

2. Look at the lunar calendar and select a date to begin your journal.

3. Create a page in your journal for each day of the month. Leave space on each page so you can write down the date, time, and moon phase, plus room to write down things you observe. For example, is the moon bright or hidden by clouds? Does it have a halo or an unusual color?

4. Add one more section for your feelings. Consider starting each journal entry with how you feel before you observe the moon, and end with how you feel after.

5. Go outside and record your observations. Here's where you'll use binoculars, if you have them. Continue the practice each night for a month.

6. Use colored pencils or markers to decorate each page.

Tip: If weather gets in your way, or if you don't have a good moon-viewing spot, check NASA's interactive map, the Daily Moon Guide, to view the moon every day of the year.

Being outside is a great counterbalance to daily life, partly because in nature there are fewer distractions. Your mind has a chance to relax when you are away from the overstimulation of noise, screens, lights, or crowds. You might find yourself daydreaming and enjoying other creative paths of thought. The next time you're feeling stressed, try lying down in the grass to watch clouds glide past overhead, or gaze out a window. Take slow, deep breaths, and just focus on the views of nature. Notice how your body feels before and after.

MAKE A MINI HABIT

USE YOUR GREEN THUMB

Commit to cultivating a new houseplant! It greens your space and improves indoor air quality. Pothos, monstera, or spider plants are good starter options, because they're not fussy about needing the perfect amount of sun. (Avoid overwatering by waiting until the soil is dry before you water them again.)

Wishing Tree

An outdoor wishing tree is made by hanging small slips of paper onto branches with string. Each paper contains a handwritten wish. What might you wish for? It's fun to think of silly ideas, but also good to consider what you may truly want for yourself, for someone you love, or for the planet. Try making your own indoor wishing tree.

What You'll Need:

Large roll of paper, such as butcher or easel paper

Construction paper in different colors

Scissors

Double-sided tape

Pencils, markers, or pens

Activity:

1. Cut a large tree trunk shape from the paper. Make it tall enough to be noticeable on a wall or door. Using the same paper, cut branch shapes.

2. Attach the tree trunk to the middle of a door or wall with tape. Attach branches all around the trunk in the shape of a tree.

3. Cut out leaves from construction paper in a variety of shapes, using green or a mix of colors.

4. Write your wishes on the leaves and attach with the tape. Stash extra blank leaves and pencils near the project, and invite anyone passing by to write a wish and attach it.

Climate Spotlight

News Flash: Cities are getting greener! Thanks to community gardens, rooftop plantings, and mini forests that can fit in small spaces, new growth is transforming many **urban** areas. This brings beautification, makes nature more accessible to everyone, and creates a chance for fun bonding in the great outdoors. How can you get involved in creating green space?

Miyawaki Forests!

Based on a **reforestation** technique from Japan, these mini forests can thrive in small areas, like a deserted corner of a school playground or a parking lot median.

Miyawaki forests grow 10 times faster than traditional reforestation efforts thanks to enriched soil and densely planted native species. For example, on a plot around the size of a basketball court, you'd plant approximately 1,400 native shrubs and saplings!

Another core concept of the mini forest movement? The planting must be done by the local community: your friends, classmates, and neighbors. The result will be a lush woodland that creates an animal habitat, absorbs **carbon dioxide** (CO_2), cleans the air, and brings people together to care for **sustainable** green space.

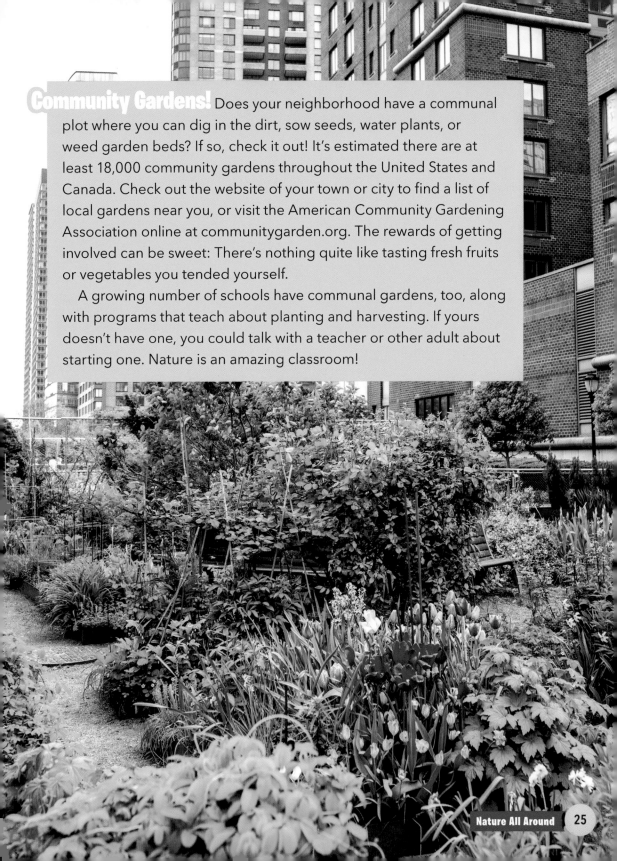

Community Gardens! Does your neighborhood have a communal plot where you can dig in the dirt, sow seeds, water plants, or weed garden beds? If so, check it out! It's estimated there are at least 18,000 community gardens throughout the United States and Canada. Check out the website of your town or city to find a list of local gardens near you, or visit the American Community Gardening Association online at communitygarden.org. The rewards of getting involved can be sweet: There's nothing quite like tasting fresh fruits or vegetables you tended yourself.

A growing number of schools have communal gardens, too, along with programs that teach about planting and harvesting. If yours doesn't have one, you could talk with a teacher or other adult about starting one. Nature is an amazing classroom!

Dream Destinations

Have you ever visited a green space in the heart of a city? There are so many interesting spaces: **reclaimed** railroads that become parks, empty lots that become community gardens, and flat urban rooftops transformed by lush plantings. They provide a calming escape from the busy streets and improve the health of the environment, too. Here are a couple of famous urban green spaces—are there any near you?

The High Line Built on a historic, elevated freight rail line, this walking trail in New York City, New York has brought beautiful nature into the heart of an urban jungle. You can stroll past native plants, grasses, shrubs, and trees to viewing decks that overlook the Hudson River and the famous Manhattan skyline. Other features include a water deck where you can get your toes wet; a raised walkway that puts you face-to-face with the treetops; and rotating displays of art, sculptures, and murals.

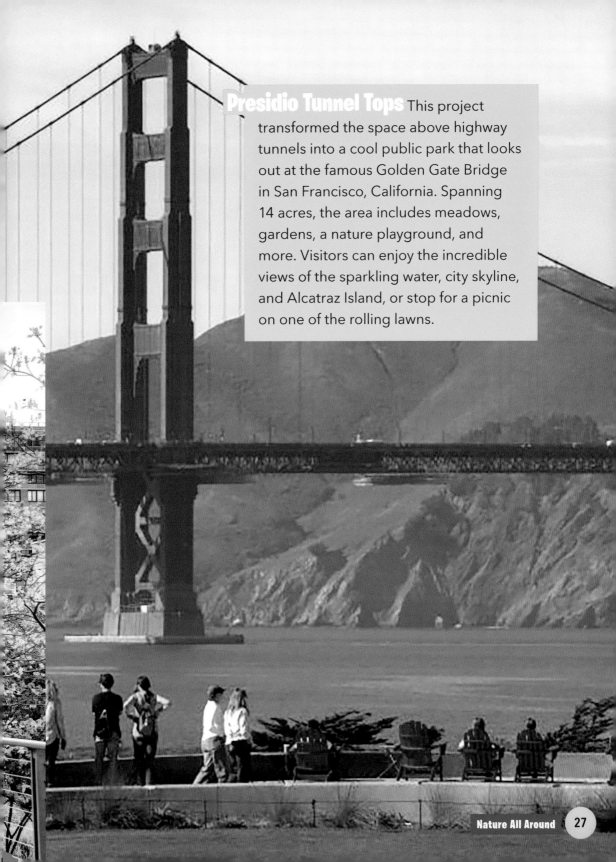

Presidio Tunnel Tops This project transformed the space above highway tunnels into a cool public park that looks out at the famous Golden Gate Bridge in San Francisco, California. Spanning 14 acres, the area includes meadows, gardens, a nature playground, and more. Visitors can enjoy the incredible views of the sparkling water, city skyline, and Alcatraz Island, or stop for a picnic on one of the rolling lawns.

CHAPTER TWO

The Big Wild

Spectacular red rock. Dark night skies that reveal the Milky Way. Towering snow-capped mountains. Glistening glacial lakes. When you're ready for the biggest adventures, it's time to look beyond the backyard and learn more about the jaw-droppingly beautiful wild places in the world.

Maybe you'll summit a peak, camp out overnight, or raft down white-water rapids. You might explore a cavern, spot a deep **gorge** or spouting **geyser,** or view magnificent wildlife. This is nature at its most stunning. For lots of people, these extraordinary interactions alight curiosity, and create a lifelong bond between them and nature in a way that benefits mind, body, and spirit.

Imagine a sight that takes your breath away: a steep canyon, a cascading waterfall; a vast snowfield on a high mountaintop that never melts, even in summer. These sights are literally "awesome"—they inspire "awe"!

What is awe, anyway? According to psychologists, it's a complex emotion linked to a sense of wonder. It's something people feel during encounters with greatness, and it stimulates your curiosity and talent for creative thinking. Experiencing awe can help us look beyond the limited scope of our life experience and be open to risk and discovery. That translates to a willingness to ask questions, try new things, and broaden your understanding of the world . . . and yourself!

Nature Mandala Making

Mandalas are intricate geometric designs, which appear across many cultures and religions, particularly Hinduism and Buddhism. Created by painting, drawing, digitally designing, or using natural materials, they are a symbol of **mindfulness**, spiritual growth, and artistic expression. Follow these steps to make your own, using objects you find outside.

What You'll Need:

- A variety of different colors, shapes, and sizes of natural materials, such as autumn leaves, stones, or wildflowers

- A flat surface to create your mandala such as a table, the ground, or a large piece of paper

Activity:

1. Take a walk outside to collect natural materials to use in your mandala.

2. Choose a design. Mandalas are circular and symmetrical, with patterns that radiate out from the center, but the colors and textures are up to you.

3. Place a leaf, stone, or flower at the center to start your mandala. Add more materials in concentric circles, working outward.

4. Turn off music and other distractions to make the process a calming and meditative experience.

5. Enjoy the stunning results of your work! If you create your mandala outside, it will be temporary, so take a photograph of your creation when you are finished.

Stars

The night sky is visible from everywhere, making it one of the most accessible parts of the natural world. Have you ever seen a shooting star? What about a planet or a constellation? Make time to gaze at the dark skies above you for a peaceful experience of wonder.

FUN FACT

The Big Dipper is part of a larger constellation called Ursa Major (the Great Bear).

Stargazing

Watching the stars is an ever-changing game, because the constellations you see differ depending on where you live, and they change as Earth rotates. If you're in an urban area where light **pollution** interferes with a clear view of space, find a planetarium near you. If you are lucky enough to have access to dark skies, follow these tips for finding two of the easiest-to-spot celestial legends.

Activity:

1. **Look for the Big Dipper.** Composed of seven bright stars, the Big Dipper has a distinct shape: a trapezoidal "bowl" of four stars and a curved "handle" of three stars. It's visible all year round in the Northern Hemisphere, but its position in the sky changes with the seasons.

2. **Look for Orion.** This constellation is supposed to be shaped like a giant hunter, named Orion. Look for Orion's Belt first: three bright stars in a nearly straight line. Two brighter stars to the north mark his shoulders, and one above those represents his head. Two more to the south of the belt represent his feet. Look for Orion between late fall and early spring in the Northern Hemisphere, or during summer in the Southern Hemisphere.

3. **Identify more constellations by printing out a star chart for the month or time you are observing.** Smartphone apps such as SkySafari or Star Walk can be helpful, but avoid looking at a bright screen while you stargaze because it will interfere with your night vision.

Being outside in the wilderness under cover of darkness lets you experience a world that you usually sleep through. Many national parks offer after-sunset programs, like supervised night hikes to learn about wild **nocturnal** animals. On a clear night without much moonlight, you might even see the Milky Way.

FUN FACT

There are more than 200 International Dark Sky Places around the world, where light pollution is regulated, and the Milky Way is visible.

SCIENCE SAYS

The Science of Night Vision

Have you ever noticed that if you remain in the dark for long enough, it gradually becomes easier to see? This is due to the amazing science of sight. Our eyes are made up of cone cells, which allow us to see colors and fine details, and rod cells, which reveal black and white and are more sensitive in low light. **Rhodopsin** is a light-sensitive receptor protein in the rods that builds up gradually when you are in the dark to improve your night vision. For humans, it takes at least 45 minutes for our eyes to fully adjust! But with just one glance at a bright flashlight beam or car headlights, the rhodopsin you built up will go away, and your eyes will revert to a state where it's hard to see in the dark.

To experience the science, try this: Adjust your eyes to the dark for at least 15 minutes. Cover one eye and turn on a light. Turn the light back off, switch which eye is covered, then open one eye at a time. Notice how differently your dark-adapted eye sees?

If you want to enjoy your after-dark eye behavior but still need illumination, dim red light is the ticket: Because of its long wavelengths, it depletes stored rhodopsin at a very slow rate. Some headlamps have a red-light feature, or you can cover the front of a flashlight with red cellophane.

Climate Spotlight

National parks aren't just for fun and recreation; they are also living laboratories. What scientists observe in these ecosystems helps them to better understand the negative impacts of climate change. It also allows them to research and develop effective strategies to help protect these special wilderness areas for future generations to enjoy.

Green Transport! Visitors collectively travel over 80 million miles inside Yosemite National Park each year. The cars they drive create traffic congestion and noise pollution and account for over 60 percent of the park's **carbon** footprint. That's why the park created a system of free shuttles to famous destinations such as Badger Pass and Mariposa Grove. As of 2020, 24 of these vehicles were diesel-electric hybrids, and two were fully electric.

Do you ever take public transit? It's a great way to reduce your carbon footprint. So are electric vehicles. Try to be creative when you need to get somewhere and imagine all the different ways you might get there besides a gas-powered car!

Climate-Adapted Buildings!

Are there any climate-adapted buildings near you, like homes with solar-powered battery backups to provide power when there is a weather-related outage? Big storms like hurricanes, along with other events like wildfires, can have major impacts on structures, including those within the national parks.

For example, the Flamingo Visitor Center and Lodge, located in the southernmost district of the 1.5-million-acre Everglades National Park in Florida, have been repeatedly demolished by hurricanes—and repeatedly rebuilt. After Hurricane Irma caused more damage in 2017, a decision was made to use climate-adaptable features for reconstruction. Reopened in 2022, the buildings are now elevated to better withstand increasingly common storm surges and are made of durable materials such as repurposed steel shipping containers.

Imagine the majesty of a huge elk or the power of a grizzly. What animal would you most like to see in the wild? Here are a few hot spots for wildlife viewing around the country where you can glimpse such creatures in their natural habitats.

Safe Wildlife Viewing

The big wild brings amazing opportunities to spot creatures in their natural habitat. It's important to learn how to view wildlife safely, so remember these handy tips:

✳ Keep your eyes peeled! If you spot an animal, remain still and quietly share the news with your group. Noise and quick movements can make wildlife feel threatened.

✳ Follow the rule of thumb: Hold your arm out straight in front of you with your thumb up. Close one eye and focus on the animal with the other. Position your thumb to cover the animal. If it's completely covered, you're at a safe distance.

✳ Aim for a distance of 25 yards from most wildlife and more than 100 yards from large wildlife.

✳ Stay on the safe side of fences and railings, and follow the rules of the specific park you are visiting.

✳ If you want a closer look, use a camera with zoom or binoculars to view animals safely.

APEX PREDATORS

In Yellowstone National Park—spanning Wyoming, Montana, and Idaho—you might see famed hunters like grizzly bears and wolves roaming near their prey. Some of the best wildlife viewing happens during winter in the Lamar Valley, where many animals take shelter.

BIG BISON

The prairies of the Wichita Mountains National Wildlife Refuge in Oklahoma helped save the American bison from **extinction**. Traveling on the reserve's roads and trails might mean sightings of bison, Rocky Mountain elk, and black-tailed prairie dogs that inhabit several "towns" in the park.

FEATHERED FRIENDS

The Aransas National Wildlife Refuge on the Texas Gulf Coast might just be the country's best place to spot birds. Over 400 different bird species have been recorded here, alongside other creatures such as sea turtles, manatees, alligators, coyotes, and bobcats.

FUN FACT

In the winter, bears enter a state of light hibernation that allows them to go for about 100 days without eating, drinking, peeing, or pooping!

How different would your morning feel if you woke up in the wilderness? Zipping open a tent door to find unspoiled nature a few inches away from your nose creates a sense of possibility and freedom that's tough to come by on a regular weekday morning.

Camping outdoors requires a little legwork, and a sense of adventure. But the effort pays off!

All your senses come alive as you see woodland creatures scamper, hear birds chirp, smell the fresh air, and (hopefully!) taste a marshmallow toasted over a flickering campfire. Getting time away from the hustle and bustle, and immersing yourself in the serenity of nature, can be a great way to relax and recharge.

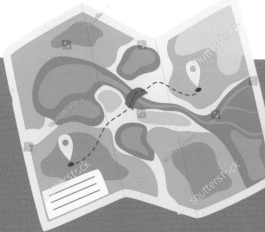

MAKE A MINI HABIT

BE A TRAIL FOLLOWER

Don't let your feet stray from the path: Stick to trails to preserve biodiversity. When you trample plants that need protecting, it can begin a cascading effect of damage that degrades the habitat of flora and fauna and alters a treasured landscape forever. Observe the sidewalks and paths in your own neighborhood to kick-start the good habit!

Fun Campout Activities

Whether you plan to camp out in a backyard, in an RV, or at a campsite, you're sure to have fun with all the activities you can enjoy outdoors. Here are some ideas to inspire you to explore from dawn to dusk—all with printable materials like game sheets and checklists you can access from the National Wildlife Federation website nwf.org.

* **Scavenger Hunt:** Make wildlife figurines using toys and crafting supplies, then hide them around your backyard or neighborhood for friends and family to hunt.

* **Bug Bingo:** Use a bug bingo sheet to have fun counting up creepy crawlies.

* **Watch Birds:** Try to spot all the feathered friends on the bird-watching checklist.

* **Flashlight Tag:** Communicate rules for staying safe, and begin play after dark.

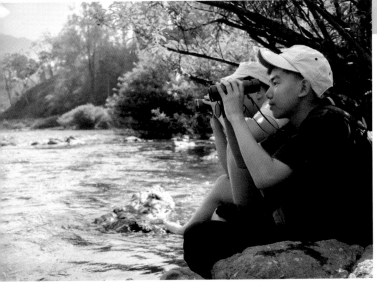

What activities in the big wild sound fun to you? Take time before your next major outdoor excursion to set a goal to try something new that appeals to you.

Research shows that setting goals you can work toward creates a sense of purpose and keeps you motivated. Achieving goals gives you something to celebrate! Here are a few ideas on how you can set your own outdoor goals.

#NatureGoals

1. **Get Specific:** Think about what you want to accomplish, making sure your goal is achievable. If you can't take yourself on vacation to Hawaii, snorkeling might not be a sensible goal. But you could set a goal to learn about tropical fish or visit a local aquarium to see marine creatures.

2. **Share Your Goal:** Tell your parents, friends, or other caring adults about your goal. Having support and encouragement can be really helpful motivation.

3. **Make Milestones:** Imagine what small steps you can take to achieve the larger goal. For example, if you want to swim across a lake, increase the minutes you swim every week to increase your stamina. If you want to spend more time in nature, try replacing one TV show a week with time outside.

4. **Reward Yourself:** As you progress toward your goal, be patient when obstacles arise. Set up rewards for achieving milestones, and make sure to celebrate when you achieve your goal!

Ideas for Outdoor Goals:

* Try a new summer sport like paddleboarding.

* Find and identify 10 kinds of leaves.

* Paddle a canoe or kayak.

* Learn to use a compass.

* Hike up a hill.

* Learn to identify a bird by its song.

* Get a great photo of a river, lake, or mountain.

* Try a new winter sport like snowshoeing.

Dream Destinations

The United States contains 63 national parks, 560 national wildlife refuges, and nearly 250 million acres of other public lands, which translates to a lot of wildernesses that you can explore. Some parks especially shine in one season, so here are highlights of when you might consider a visit.

FALL

Acadia National Park Maine is beautiful in summer, but the quieter fall season is a dream. The park's scenic coastal hikes, bike rides along forested roads, stunning lakes, and rocky shorelines are free of crowds and open for exploration, with a backdrop of gorgeous bright fall **foliage**.

WINTER
Bryce Canyon National Park
This rugged landscape of red rock dusted with snow in winter is one of Utah's stunning, not-to-be-missed sights. Take a winter hike, strap on cross-country skis, or attend the annual Bryce Canyon Winter Festival that happens on Presidents' Day weekend each year.

SPRING
Joshua Tree National Park
Did you know that wildflowers bloom in the California desert? Visit this park in spring to see an amazing spread of colorful blossoms that only last until the intense heat of summer takes over.

SUMMER
North Cascades National Park
Discover the unforgettable mountain views, dense evergreen forests, and crystal-clear lakes of the alpine wilderness in Washington State. The summer days in the northwest are longer than most, offering extra hours for exploring, hiking, birding, and camping.

CHAPTER THREE

Water

Whether you hike a rocky shoreline, jump into waves at the beach, or explore a creek on a sunny day, spending time near lakes, rivers, ponds, and oceans equals fun and adventure. Research also shows that being around water helps you feel calm and improves your sense of well-being.

Clean, healthy waterways are key to every part of life on Earth, from supplying drinking water to providing for wildlife on land and in the skies overhead. Water takes so many forms, from rain and snow to glaciers. Learning more about how to protect this vital resource is as important as remembering to go outside and enjoy it!

Being around water can help you unwind and relax when the world feels busy or overwhelming. Why? Because H_2O provides information for your brain to process, about what you see, hear, touch, and smell. Another way of saying this is that water offers a lot of "sensory input." Interpreting the world through our senses distracts our minds from stressful thoughts and allows us to focus on the present moment.

Can you think of moments when water engages your senses? A list might include some of these:

* hearing the crash of waves

* seeing your **reflection** in a puddle

* touching a river current

* smelling the salty ocean

Monterey Canyon, an underwater gorge off the central coast of California, is about as deep as the Grand Canyon!

SCIENCE SAYS

Out of the Blue

Bodies of water such as oceans, seas, and lakes are sometimes called "blue space." But why are they blue? The explanation lies in the science of light, which moves as waves of different lengths. Some waves, like those at the red end of the spectrum, are longer, while others, like blue waves, are shorter. When sunlight hits the water, the water molecules absorb the longer red wavelengths more easily, while the shorter blue wavelengths penetrate more deeply. This process of "selective absorption" results in the beautiful color of the ocean.

Research shows that the more time people spend near water, the better they feel. The benefits can include an increased sense of calm and reduced stress. Luckily, you don't have to engineer a perfect day at the beach to enjoy the happy effects of being near water. You don't even have to be outside: Studies show that being near any kind of water can help. (Yes, even just looking at a fish tank!) What are some interesting or unexpected aquatic destinations near you? Here are a few ideas to get you started:

River * Fish tank * Ocean * Boardwalk * City fountain * Pond * Canal * Aquarium * Creek * Waterfall

FUN FACT

Waterfalls can create their own weather! The plunging water releases mist that cools the air nearby, creating localized cloud formations and even rainbows.

Relax to Water Sounds

Soft pattering rain. Ocean waves lapping the sand. The gentle splash of a fountain. The soothing sounds created by water form the basis for this five-minute relaxation activity. Follow these steps to reduce stress and clear your mind.

1. **Tune In:** Find a spot outside where you can hear water sounds, staying away from noisy distractions and screens. If you need to be inside, relax near a window on a rainy day or play soothing water sounds on a speaker. Start a five-minute timer.

2. **Notice Your Breath:** Take five deep breaths, then continue breathing in a way that feels natural and relaxed. Gently close your eyes if you like. Focus on the present moment.

3. **Open Your Ears:** Listen to the water sounds and notice any shifts in rhythm or volume. Follow this mindful practice as you continue your relaxed breathing.

4. **Notice How You Feel:** When the timer goes off, take a final deep breath and gently open your eyes. Notice how you feel. Are you more relaxed than when you started? Try this with different water sounds, and see how the experience changes.

Have you ever felt like you could spend hours digging holes in wet sand and watching them fill with ocean water? Or cleared away sticks and debris in a creek to allow the water to flow more freely? Interacting with dynamic aspects of water such as currents, tides, and waves ignites your imagination and inspires experimentation.

FUN FACT

The powerful, narrow channels of water that move quickly away from shore called rip currents can travel more than five miles per hour, faster than an Olympic swimmer.

Water Lily Float

With some easy folding, you can make a simple origami water lily. Explore a nearby creek or stream by setting the flower on the water's surface to investigate the currents. Don't forget to take your water lily with you when you're done!

What You'll Need:

> 7 x 7-inch square paper such as origami paper
>
> clear tape

Activity:

1. Fold your square piece of paper diagonally one way, then the other diagonal way. Unfold.

2. Fold in the corners to the middle where the diagonal creases intersect.

3. Fold the corners two more times.

4. Fold the outermost flaps out partway. Do the same with the other two sets of flaps, creasing them well to make sure they stand up.

5. Reinforce the corners and the bottom with clear tape to keep your water lily dry. Now you are ready to launch your flower.

1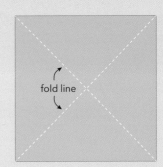
fold line

2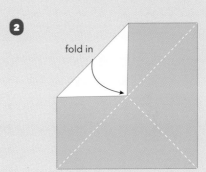
fold in

3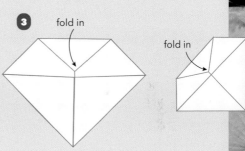
fold in   fold in

4
fold out   fold out

Climate Spotlight

Climate change and pollution are creating challenges for our planet's oceans in the form of rising sea levels, which cause habitat destruction, and plastic debris that hurts marine life. As important as it is to understand problems, however, remember to focus on solutions as well!

For example, protecting waterways from plastic waste can make a big difference. More than 11 million metric tons of plastics end up in the ocean each year. And that's on top of the estimated 200 million metric tons that are already there. The litter comes from bags, bottles, and straws; equipment used for offshore fishing and aquaculture; and microplastics from things like the film around pods of laundry detergent. It's a big issue to tackle, but innovators and conservationists are finding creative new ways to make changes—and your actions, even small ones, can have a positive impact.

Group Power! Organizations like the Ocean Conservancy are devoted to fighting for trash-free seas. With the help of volunteers, the group has picked up more than 348 million pounds of trash in the past 35 years. Check out their International Coastal Cleanup initiative to find a cleanup planned in your region.

Jellyfish Robots! Inspired by the swift and efficient movements of jellyfish in the water, scientists in Germany created an energy-efficient and quiet robot called Jellyfish-Bot. The machine circulates water like a real jellyfish and can move through the ocean collecting plastic or waste particles. Then it transports the litter to the surface for **recycling**. For you, the process is a little easier than it is for the robot: On land, all you need to do is walk to the closest recycling bin that takes glass, plastic, or paper!

FUN FACT

Nearly half of all ocean pollution comes from activities that take place on land.

Super Seaweed! If you think seaweed is just something that washes up on the beach, think again. A new technology company called Sway, based in California, is creating plastic substitutes made with seaweed that may eventually replace things like plastic packaging and cling film. Unlike plastic, seaweed biodegrades quickly, and growing it drains CO_2 from the atmosphere. Until alternatives like seaweed packaging are more widely available, try limiting your own use of kitchen plastics: Instead of using plastic baggies to store snacks, use **biodegradable** waxed paper or reusable containers.

NATURAL WONDER

Snow and Rain

Have you ever seen falling snow and admired the beauty of slowly cascading flakes? It might have given you a sense of peace to see nature transformed by that fluffy blanket of white. This frozen water brings magic to a long winter and makes it fun to get outside despite the cold.

Build Snölykta

With plenty of snow on hand, you can make a snölykta (glowing snowball lantern) and light up the night. Building snölykta is a cold weather tradition in Sweden, where it's popular to go outside no matter the weather. As the saying goes, "There is no such thing as bad weather, just bad clothes!"

What You'll Need:

Snow

Battery-powered lights (string lights, a headlamp, or LED tea light candles)

Activity:

1. Find a flat, snowy area.

2. Pack snow into about 25 tight snowballs.

3. Make a small circle of about 8–10 snowballs.

4. Pile more snowballs on your initial circle to make a hollow pyramid with a hole at the top.

5. Put lights inside and turn them on.

6. Close the top with the final snowballs.

7. Step back and enjoy the beauty of lights in the snow!

Winter Rain Painting

Snow might be scarce where you live. But even warm places might have "winter weather" in the form of wind and rain. This craft is perfect for making during a downpour.

What You'll Need:

Watercolor paint cakes

Paper

Art trays or 9 x 12-inch baking sheets

Paper bag, bowl, or wax paper

Plastic wrap

Activity:

1. Pop the paint cakes from the container, place in a paper bag, a bowl or even between two sheets of wax paper (any way to contain a mess!), and break into small pieces.

2. Place your paper in the tray and decorate with bits of paint.

3. Set the tray outside where falling raindrops will make the colors run and mix.

4. If the watercolors don't run and bleed, layer plastic wrap or wax paper over the paper and squish it in by hand.

5. Lay your painting on a dry tray for it to dry.

One thing that makes large bodies of water extra special is what's next to them: the beach. These strips of sand form when natural forces like wind, rain, and pounding waves break down gravel and rock into tiny particles, which are deposited along shorelines.

Sand comes in lots of different colors! Brown or white sand is most common, made of tiny particles of rock and pulverized minerals such as quartz and mica. Black sand colored by hardened lava is found in Hawaii and other places with volcanic activity. You can spot rare pink sand made of coral reefs and shells in tropical spots like Bermuda.

Sandcastle Serenity

Working with sand becomes a meditative activity if you observe a mindful approach, working slowly and engaging all your senses. If you can't get to a beach, fill a bin with kinetic sand instead, which is easily moldable and fun to work with indoors.

What You'll Need:

Large shovel and large bucket

Small shovels and buckets

Spoons, mini rakes, trowels, or fun-shaped containers

Activity:

1. Take a peaceful beach walk to gather decorations for your castle: seashells, seaweed, or sticks. Choose a site for your castle.

2. Walk near the water's edge and test the sand beneath your fingers. What consistency will work best for packing solid walls?

3. Bring big buckets of sand to your area and think creatively about what might make your castle unique. Will you dig a trench around the walls to form a moat, add lookout towers, or draw designs along the walls?

4. Focus on the different objects you collected on your beach walk. What interesting ways can you use them to decorate your castle? When it's time to head home, leave your sandcastle and special beach finds where they belong, in their natural habitat.

Do you have any favorite water activities?
Here are a few fun ones to try:

WATERFALL HIKING

The crashing churn of a waterfall is an exciting sight—and hiking to reach one is so much fun. Found everywhere from mountains and hills to forests and canyons, these natural wonders can be found in any region with rugged landscapes, abundant rainfall, and accessible rivers. Do some research to find one near you. An alternative is to check out man-made destinations, like large dams, or waterfall installations at urban parks.

TUBING

For a fun time, it's hard to beat tubing—and there are two very different kinds! In free-floating, or river, tubing, riders glide along the natural current of a river for a peaceful experience. Towed tubing is an exhilarating thrill ride where tube riders tethered to a motorboat are pulled at high speeds around a large lake or wide river. As with all watersports, tubers must wear gear like life vests and helmets and have adult supervision at all times.

POLAR PLUNGING

Just because it's cold doesn't mean you have to stay inside! A polar plunge is a group event where everyone braves a dip in chilly water together, usually held in the winter. You might even see people walking across snow before swimming! In Maryland, the annual Cool Schools Plunge brings students together for a cold plunge outing. Do some research to find out about polar plunges in your area—a lot of them are fundraisers for great causes!

MAKE A MINI HABIT

CARRY REUSABLE CONTAINERS

Choose a sturdy lunch box, reusable water bottle, and travel mug that you can wash and reuse. This allows you to use and discard less packaging like plastic bags, bottles, foam cups, and straws, which often end up polluting our streams, rivers, and oceans.

SCIENCE SAYS

Have You Heard of . . . Cenotes?

These natural sinkholes form when limestone bedrock collapses to expose groundwater beneath, resulting in extraordinary crystal-clear pools. Cenotes can be found around the world, although Mexico's Yucatán Peninsula might be the most famous place to see them. Considered sacred by the ancient Mayans of the area, larger cenotes often feature underground caves, unique rock formations, and diverse marine life. Visitors from around the world are drawn to them for swimming, diving, exploration, and contemplation.

Dream Destinations

More than 70 percent of Earth's surface is covered with water, in the form of oceans, lakes, rivers, glaciers, and more. Humans have explored only a tiny fraction of that. What types of water destinations have you explored? How adventurous do you like to be? Maybe your newest #naturegoal is one of the trips listed here, or maybe you can imagine something even better!

Raft a River The serenity of floating along a peaceful river becomes the adventure of a lifetime as soon as you encounter churning rapids! That's where experienced guides come in, helping visitors of all ages navigate white water on trips along rivers with famous rapids. Some of the best destinations for group trips are Idaho's spectacular Salmon River; the Flathead River in Montana; the Youghiogheny River, winding through West Virginia, Pennsylvania, and Maryland; and the Nantahala River in western North Carolina.

Snorkel Tropical Waters

Swimming among bright tropical fish is a magical experience. Amazing destinations to snorkel are the Hawaiian islands, including Kauai, Maui, and Oahu; the crystalline waters of Cozumel, Mexico; and Belize, home to the largest barrier reef system in the Northern Hemisphere, where you can spot vibrant marine life and coral formations.

Visit a Volcanic Lake

Lakes formed by volcanic activity are famous for their purity and crystal-blue color. See one for yourself with a visit to Crater Lake in Oregon, the deepest lake in the United States, which formed after a volcano erupted about 7,500 years ago. Other stunning destinations include Lake Tahoe, the largest alpine lake in North America that's located in California and Nevada, and Yellowstone Lake in Wyoming, uniquely located at the high elevation of 7,730 feet above sea level.

CHAPTER FOUR
Trees

Being around trees is great for your state of mind: Studies show that as little as 15 minutes of walking in a forest can improve your mood and relieve stress and anxiety. In fact, according to research, even just the sight of green rustling leaves on trees out a window promotes increased relaxation.

Beyond making you feel better, trees keep the planet healthy by tackling all kinds of issues: They curb air pollution, contribute to cleaner water, provide essential animal habitats, and cool cities (which, due to an abundance of dark roofs and paved streets and a lack of green space, can become "heat islands"). Trees also help combat climate change by absorbing harmful CO_2: One tree can sequester (or take in) more than one ton of carbon dioxide in its lifetime. The easy activities in this chapter will inspire you to find more reasons to spend time among trees, where you can appreciate and enjoy everything they have to offer.

What are your first memories of interacting with trees?
You might remember the first time you climbed branches, spotted
an animal in the woods, or jumped in a pile of autumn leaves. What
about the last time you felt dwarfed by a massive trunk with branches
towering far overhead? Trees like this inspire a sense of awe: Not only
are they huge, these organisms are among the oldest on Earth.

Get to know the trees around you by learning what grows in your area.
Can you adopt a special tree in a nearby park or your own backyard?
Here are some ideas for how you can get to know your tree:

* Sit below your tree with closed eyes and make notes
  afterward of wind sounds or birdsong.

* Sketch your tree in spring, summer, fall, and winter
  to notice how it changes. Watch for creatures like
  squirrels and birds and track their activity.

* Lie beneath your tree and look upward through the
  branches.

* Visit your tree often with a notebook and jot down
  how it has changed since your last visit.

Methuselah,
North America's oldest
bristlecone pine tree, is
nearly 5,000 years old!

SCIENCE SAYS

Tree Talk

Even if you can't hear trees chatting when you walk
in the woods, did you know they are having a kind of
conversation? Science shows that while trees might not
speak your language, they do communicate. Through their roots,
trees communicate with the forest around them by connecting with
large networks of underground fungi. This creates what's known as a
mycorrhizal network (*myco* means fungus, *rhizal* means root) where
chemical signals are exchanged between different types of trees and
plants. These "conversations" can lead to the sharing of resources
like nutrients and water! Scientists are really interested in this,
because future discoveries may have big impacts, like finding ways to
enrich soil so crops are more plentiful.

Peaceful rustling leaves and active wildlife exist just about anywhere a tree puts down roots. A hike in the woods is a terrific way to enjoy yourself: As you make progress on a trail, don't forget to enjoy a water break in the shade, scramble on fallen logs or low branches, and keep an eye out for adorable woodland creatures!

Build a Hike

Build a custom plan for a hike that suits your interests and abilities with these tips.

Plan Your Route

Choose what type of hike you want to take. Are you looking for an adventurous trail that rises to the top of the **tree line** or a peaceful lap on a paved path in the shade? Do you want to pack a lunch and be gone all day, or finish your trek in an hour?

Add a Goal

Set a hiking goal you can measure, like time spent, steps taken, or elevation gained. Then add to it each time you lace up your boots! Try taking an annual hike on your birthday and extending it by 10 minutes each year: A 20-minute hike when you're eight will extend to an hour-long hike by age 12! Accomplishing goals is a great confidence-booster.

Design a Loop

Some trails take you there and back, especially in the mountains! But it can be more rewarding to hike a loop trail instead, getting new views around every corner. Check the map next time you hike and look for trails that connect in a circular route.

Scavenger Hunt for Sounds

See how quietly you can move through the woods, or even take time to sit and listen and track what noises you hear. Maybe it's the cry of a hawk or the hammer of a woodpecker. Are your footsteps crunchy or soft? Is the wind a howl or a whisper? Nature has a soundtrack of its own if you tune in.

Fall

Have you ever picked an apple or pear from a tree? Autumn is a special time of year because it brings harvest, when orchards bear fruit. What grows on trees and farms near you in the fall? It's always a beautiful time to be outside, as the weather cools and leaves turn red and gold.

Visit an orchard or farm to deepen your connection with what you eat and maybe try harvesting with your own hands. Celebrate the season with a local fall festival, or stop by a farmers market to taste items harvested from farms nearby.

DIY Recipe Box

Just like doing your own harvesting, many people find cooking relaxing—and the results are delicious! Just like doing your own harvesting, cooking results in something delicious! Make this easy craft to keep track of your favorite recipes.

What You'll Need:

Shoebox

Colorful wrapping paper

Index cards (4 x 6 inches)

Double-sided tape

Activity:

1. Find a shoebox that you can repurpose. Look for a smaller, kid-sized shoebox of about 7 inches long. You want the index cards to easily fit inside. If you use a larger box, ask for an adult's help with cutting it down to size.

2. Use decorative paper to wrap the exterior of the box, attaching it with double-sided tape. Cut out more paper, in a contrasting color or pattern if you like, to cover the bottom of the box on the inside.

3. Write down your favorite recipes on the index cards and decorate them with drawings or stickers. Stash the cards inside the box and organize by season: strawberry or asparagus recipes in spring; corn or blackberry recipes in summer; squash or cranberry recipes in fall and winter, for example.

Eighty percent of Earth's land animals and plants live in forests. But not all forests are the same! Take this moment to get acquainted with a few major types of forests and what makes each one unique:

CONIFEROUS FOREST

Thin, needlelike leaves make the evergreen trees in this type of forest easy to recognize. Look for spruces, pines, and firs bearing cones, some of which can grow to be over a foot long. Different types of coniferous forests grow in many diverse environments, from mountains and northern forests to the warmer climates of the south or the arid plateaus of the high desert.

DECIDUOUS FOREST

Look for maple, oak, beech, and other trees characterized by color-changing foliage in the fall. The leaves come in varying sizes and shapes, from broad and smooth to oval or elongated and jagged. This type of forest is found just about everywhere with moist summers and cold winters.

F UN FACT

The world's largest rainforest is the Amazon in South America. It covers as much land as the 48 contiguous U.S. states.

RAINFOREST

These dense forests get approximately 70 to almost 400 inches of rainfall per year and come in two types. Temperate rainforests lie in coastal areas with mild temperatures, like the Pacific Northwest, where the towering trees include coastal redwood and giant sequoia. Tropical rainforests thrive closer to the equator where temperatures remain warm all year, and the tree variety includes Brazil nut, rubber, and kapok trees.

Leaf Rubbing

Have you ever noticed that some leaves have pointy edges while others are smooth? Or how the base of a leaf has a different shape than the tip? Slow down to really examine the details and make some beautiful art.

What You'll Need:

> Newly fallen leaves (not too dry or brittle)
>
> Large piece of paper (not too thick)
>
> Wax crayons or pastels

Activity:

1. Collect fallen leaves in different sizes and shapes (larger ones with noticeable texture often work best). Position one leaf on a flat surface. Spread your paper flat over it.

2. Gently rub the side of the crayon up and down on the paper until the shape and texture of the leaf emerge. Use light, even pressure and focus on the edges.

3. Start with dark colors to best reveal the texture. Do multiple leaf rubbings, comparing different varieties. Find your favorite shapes and try fitting them together in a kind of interlocking puzzle, like what you might see on a forest floor blanketed with leaves.

4. Experiment with using other colors. Use four or five different shades on a single piece of paper for a multicolored result. Turn your creations into homemade cards or hang them to make an art wall.

When you relax beneath a tree in the summer, you count on its green foliage for shade—but those leaves are also essential for much more. They contribute to the very existence of life on Earth! How? Because the same leaves cooling you off make the air you breathe: Oxygen is a byproduct of photosynthesis, the process where plants use sunlight to turn CO_2 and water into glucose (sugar), which is their energy source.

As leaves fall from trees, they also create a habitat on the ground for countless creatures, from salamanders and turtles to moths and bats. And leaves are an important part of human history: Ancient manuscripts were written on palm leaves, and cultures all over the world use various leaves for cooking!

Climate Spotlight

You might have heard about deforestation: That's when forests are cut down to log, clear space for plantations, develop cities, and more. It's worrying to think that more forest land is being cleared every hour, destroying habitats for many creatures. But there are positive changes being made, like people getting involved with tree planting to create a positive impact on this climate issue. And you can learn about the efforts and technologies working to combat deforestation and protect the millions of species who call forests home.

A Trillion New Trees! Trees are the lungs of our planet. They trap carbon, a pollutant that contributes to **global warming**, and store it safely in their wood, which aids our environment. Important progress against deforestation is being made by groups like Tree-Nation, who work to plant more trees every year. Their ambitious goal? To plant one trillion new trees on Earth by 2050. Can you think of a place to plant a tree?

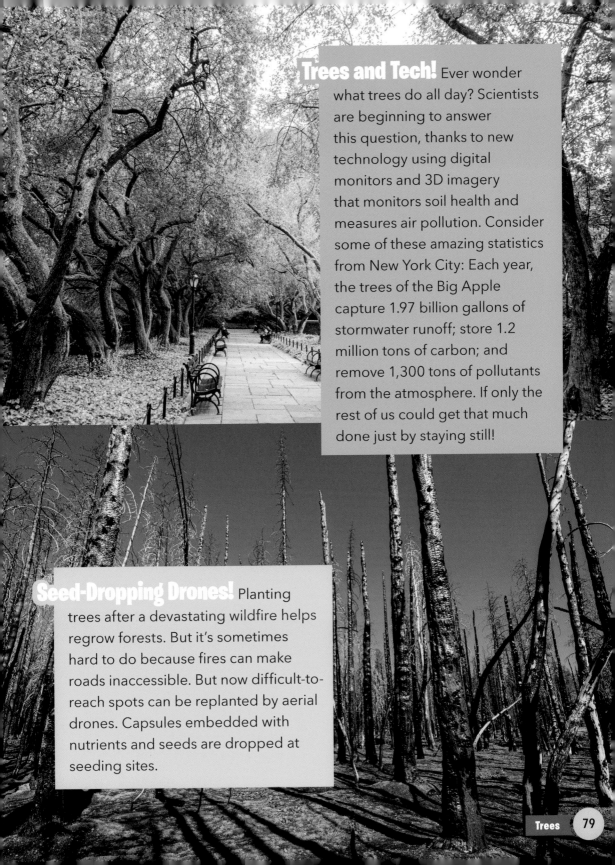

Trees and Tech! Ever wonder what trees do all day? Scientists are beginning to answer this question, thanks to new technology using digital monitors and 3D imagery that monitors soil health and measures air pollution. Consider some of these amazing statistics from New York City: Each year, the trees of the Big Apple capture 1.97 billion gallons of stormwater runoff; store 1.2 million tons of carbon; and remove 1,300 tons of pollutants from the atmosphere. If only the rest of us could get that much done just by staying still!

Seed-Dropping Drones! Planting trees after a devastating wildfire helps regrow forests. But it's sometimes hard to do because fires can make roads inaccessible. But now difficult-to-reach spots can be replanted by aerial drones. Capsules embedded with nutrients and seeds are dropped at seeding sites.

Imagine walking along a wooded trail in the summer, sunlight filtering down through the glowing green canopy of leaves while birds chirp. Of all the many amazing activities you can do outside, a walk in the woods might relax you the most, whether it's in your backyard, local park, or an actual forest. Does that surprise you?

Research shows that you feel more physically and emotionally balanced in green spaces. As a result, you may feel increased positivity, reduced stress, and a renewed ability to focus after spending time among the trees.

MAKE A MINI HABIT

USE FABRIC SHOPPING BAGS

In the United States, over 10 billion paper bags are consumed each year, requiring the felling of 14 million trees. Take notice of the types of bags and packaging you use. Carry a reusable bag with you, maybe one made of fabric that folds up very small for easy storage. When you use it instead of paper bags, you will be doing the forests a favor!

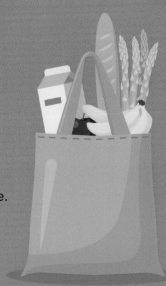

Forest Bathing

Forest bathing, known as *shinrin-yoku* in Japan, where it first originated, is a slow and purposeful engagement with nature. Unlike hiking or a nature walk, which focus on movement, a destination, or maybe finding plants and animals, forest bathing is about being calm and present in your wooded surroundings.

What You'll Need:

Comfortable shoes   A water bottle and sunscreen

Plenty of time

Activity:

1. Turn off devices and put them away. Turn on your senses so you can be mindful of everything in the woods around you.

2. Set a time goal. Start with a short 15-minute forest bathing walk if it's not realistic to do an hour-long experience.

3. With an adult, walk slowly and quietly through the woods, or find a good place to sit. Bring awareness to your senses. Focus on shapes you see, sounds you hear, and the scents around you. Take long breaths deep into your belly and exhale slowly.

4. Become aware of your body in space and stay in the present moment. Keep a peaceful silence if you are walking with friends or family, and speak up only if you have an important observation to share.

5. End your forest bathing and check in with yourself. Are your thoughts calmer? Is your body more relaxed? Research shows that forest bathing has health benefits that range from reducing stress hormones to improving your sleep at night.

Trees provide habitats for birds and animals, giving them shelter and protection from predators and harsh weather. Have you ever spotted a nest or a burrow in the woods? The next time you are outside, follow these tips and you might get lucky:

✳ **Watch for small movements:** Tiny motions, like the shifting of branches on a bush or the slight bounce of a tree branch, can tip you off that an animal is nearby.

✳ **Try binoculars:** Ask an adult for binoculars so you can see distant or high-up nests more clearly.

✳ **Listen with active ears:** Bird calls, the quiet rustle of leaves, or the sound of skittering gravel can all indicate that woodland creatures are not far.

FUN FACT

Bald eagles can soar over 10,000 feet high and spot fish up to a mile away.

Habitat Matching

A wide range of species lives on the forest floor and in the various microhabitats trees offer, like the treetops, roots, and trunks (especially hollow ones). Can you match the animal to the habitat where it lives?

Great Bald Eagle
This majestic hunter builds large nests near bodies of water and uses its keen eyesight to hunt for food.

Forest Floor

Chipmunks
These adorable critters often burrow a series of tunnels that follow along one particular area of a tree.

Hollow Trunk

Spring Peepers
Small tree frogs that are rarely seen but often heard, these little guys like marshy woods and blend in easily with fallen leaves. In spring the males' high-pitched whistling or peeping sound is repeated about 20 times a minute.

Treetops

Great Horned Owl
This nocturnal animal doesn't actually have horns, but rather tufts of feathers on either side of its head, along with an impressive wingspan of about 4.5 feet!

Tree Roots

Great bald eagle and treetops. Chipmunks and tree roots. Spring peepers and forest floor. Great horned owl and hollow trunk.

Dream Destinations

Forests cover about 30 percent of Earth's land surface, ranging from rainforests to deciduous forests. How many kinds of forests have you explored? Start your own wish list of incredible forests you want to learn about or experience! Here a few ideas to get you started:

White Mountain National Forest Spanning more than 800,000 acres, this destination in New Hampshire and Maine is known for its spectacular trees and the craggy mountains of the Presidential Range. Take a cog railway or drive to the top of the 6,288-foot Mount Washington. From this peak, you get views of seemingly endless woods.

Aspen Groves Quaking aspen possess an extremely unique trait. In the fall, groves with thousands of trees all turn gold at exactly the same time. That's because all the individual trees in the grove are part of the same root system. . . making them basically all function as one. Visit one of Colorado's famous aspen groves or head to Utah, home to a remarkable quaking aspen grove called Pando, which some scientists think is the largest living land organism in the world!

Tongass National Forest Alaska is home to this massive forest of nearly 17 million acres, more than half as big as the entire state of North Carolina. Trees, including massive Sitka spruce, western hemlock, and cedar, combine with geological features like majestic glaciers and ice fields to create a unique landscape.

CHAPTER FIVE

Relaxing Outdoor Rituals

What are your favorite ways to recharge outside?
You might already have habits that help you relax, like watching the
sunset, hiking a wooded trail, or sitting quietly on the shores of a lake.
Turning to nature to reduce stress and renew your sense of calm can
be effective and easy.

If you're looking for new and interesting outdoor rituals to add
to your routine, this chapter will come in handy. Think of these as
planned moments that motivate you to enjoy the sights and sounds of
nature. Creating new habits that help you interact with and appreciate
the world around you is a great skill, one that will contribute to your
overall well-being now, and for the rest of your life!

You might have regular activities that take you outside every day, like waiting at the bus stop each morning or walking a pet after school. What if you added a just-for-fun outdoor ritual to your schedule?

This new habit might be something as simple as opening the window to take five deep breaths of fresh air every morning or devoting 10 minutes to taking a walk before dinner. Brainstorm fun ideas on your own or try something that brings fellow nature lovers together, like the next activity on page 89.

Follow strategies to set yourself up for success, like choosing a specific time each day, week, or month to observe your new ritual. Set a reminder alarm, if you like. It can also help to find a buddy who helps you stay on track with your goals. Having someone to cheer you on when you're creating a new habit can make a big difference in achieving success—and you can return the favor, encouraging them to do their best and meet their goals as well!

Start a Sunset-Watching Club

A social club based on shared interests can be really fun—and a great way to meet new friends or spend more time with people you already love. Why not start a club for watching gorgeous sunsets together as a group? Here are four steps to make your club successful.

Activity:

1. **Set Goals:** How many sunsets do you want to catch per week? Per month? Will your club include other elements, like taking sunset photos, a volunteer list for snacks and drinks, or sunset-related art or science activities?

2. **Research and Plan:** Find out what time of day the sunset happens, and check the weather to make sure it will be visible. Map out nearby locations that are accessible and offer good viewing opportunities.

3. **Recruit and Schedule:** See who among your friends and family is interested in joining your club. Communicate clearly about when you want to schedule events and where the club will meet.

4. **Enjoy and Adapt:** Host your first club meeting. Ask members for feedback or ideas to encourage their participation. Above all, enjoy the sunset!

An outdoor ritual doesn't have to require a lot of planning! It can be really simple, like eating your lunch outside, or doing 20 minutes of sunset yoga. Deciding how to spend free time outside can be an enjoyable challenge, and every season will bring different opportunities. Whether you opt for a ritual that's sporty and active or something more quiet and contemplative, the main thing is to step away from technology and screens—and make time to step out the front door.

Cloud Watching Picnic

Add this cloud identification activity to a summer picnic and try it several times throughout the season. It's a treat to watch the beautiful, constantly shifting clouds and contemplate the majestic forces of wind that help create them.

Activity:

1. Choose an outdoor location where you can bring food and have an unobstructed view of the sky overhead.

2. Schedule your outing when there is plenty of time to stay and watch the clouds shift and change.

3. Pack your picnic along with a tablecloth, sheet, or blanket to lie down on.

4. Lie down and look up (never look directly at the sun, because it can harm your eyes). What shapes do you see? Can you identify any of these types of clouds?

cumulus—big, fluffy white clouds with cotton-ball rounding at the edges and flat bottoms

altocumulus–midlevel clouds that often appear as white streaks; similar to stratocumulus, but with smaller clouds

stratocumulus–rippling low-lying clouds that blanket the sky in different shades of gray

cumulonimbus–storm clouds that bring heavy snow or rain with a large fluffy cap like a mushroom, also called "thunderheads"

cirrus–wispy clouds at high altitudes

altocumulus lenticularis–clouds that form near mountain peaks and have a unique appearance due to the high winds that form them

The phrase "finding balance" is about more than staying upright as you walk on top of a fallen log or stepping stones. When it comes to life, finding balance is when you feel like the parts of your life work together easily.

For example, if you experience lots of stress and little relaxation, it can affect your sleep, your mood, and your learning. But not all "stress" is bad—if you only relax and never tackle a challenge, you won't learn important things or develop new skills. Achieving a good balance between stress and relaxation is important to feel your best.

Balance Building

Here are ideas to improve both your physical and mental balance— and have fun while you're at it!

PHYSICAL BALANCE
Build up your balance and agility with these easy ideas!

Outside:

* Walk along a fallen log without falling off; start with your arms extended on either side, then drop them and keep them by your sides. Is one way easier or harder?

* Step from rock to rock across a stream without getting your shoes wet.

* At the beach, make evenly spaced footprints in the sand.

Inside:

* Set one foot on a ball, then move the ball in all different directions without letting it roll out of reach.

* Put down a long line of painter's tape on the floor. Walk along it using heel-to-toe steps. After you go forward, try walking in reverse, always keeping your feet on the tape.

✳ Create an unstable surface by setting a pillow or cushion on the floor. Try to balance standing on one foot.

MENTAL BALANCE
Try these ideas to maintain your mental sense of balance.

✳ Balance indoor activities with outdoor time: After a day in the classroom, take a nature walk, or plan a meetup with friends at a park to enjoy the fresh air.

✳ When you look at your schedule, are there jam-packed days? If so, is there an activity you can move to another time? Try to schedule a day with free time after a busy one so you can relax.

✳ How can you balance energetic activities with restorative ones? Consider following a tiring activity like sports practice with a restful one, like time devoted to watching a peaceful sunset.

Bird Migration

Spring and fall bring a showstopping spectacle to the skies of North America: billions of birds migrating across the country. If you spot a small flock nibbling berries from a bush on an autumn day, it's probably feathered friends snacking on their long-haul flight. Bird-watching is a beautiful and calming way to spend time in nature, so be sure to add it to your list of relaxing outdoor rituals!

MAKE A MINI HABIT

TURN OFF THE LIGHTS!

Did you know that most migratory birds travel at night? It's true! Many scientists believe that birds prefer cooler, less windy evening conditions and even use the stars for directions. Unfortunately, brightly lit windows at night confuse birds, throwing them off their migratory paths and making them prone to collisions. With one flick of a switch, you can contribute to darker skies and safer passage for migrating birds. Get acquainted with the Audobon's Lights Out Program to find out more.

Upcycled Birdbath

Visit a thrift store near you to find items you can upcycle into a birdbath. Look for planter pots in different sizes and one saucer. Or, try to find similarly shaped items that can be stacked, like a ceramic vase, a mixing bowl, and a pie plate.

What You'll Need:

   Two or three sturdy items in different sizes that can stack easily on top of each other, such as planter pots or old vases

   One shallow bowl or planter pot saucer a few inches larger than the smallest pot

   Non-toxic paint

   Weatherproof glue

Activity:

1. Turn one of the planter pots upside down. Stack the second pot on top of it, then the third one if you have it. If using items such as vases, stack them to create a balanced shape. Place the shallow bowl or pot saucer on top.

2. Be creative! Try different designs: As long as the pieces fit snugly and can be glued together, it will work.

3. If you have planter pots, you can paint them and set them out to dry. If you thrifted items for the project made from shiny glazed ceramic or smooth glass, there's no need!

4. Get the help of an adult to use permanent weatherproof glue to attach the pieces together. Once it's dry, fill up the birdbath with water (no deeper than two inches for bird safety), and watch feathered friends flock to your new creation!

Have you ever spotted mushrooms sprouting on a log? Picked up acorns beneath a tree? Then you know how much fun it can be to forage—or in other words, hunt for food and resources in the wild.

The ancient practice of gathering edible plants, nuts, and fungi helped early humans survive and became a cornerstone of many Indigenous populations as knowledge passed from one generation to the next. Today, modern foragers see the practice as a way to explore and connect with nature and learn more about what's edible (and poisonous!) in the wild.

FUN FACT

Wild ramps, with a flavor similar to garlic and onions, have been a popular foraged food in rural areas for decades. But recently, they've become popular in fine-dining circles as well!

TIPS FOR FORAGERS:

Get started on your foraging journey with these important guidelines.

1. **Safety First:** Always forage with the help of a knowledgeable adult. Don't plan to consume anything you forage on your own, since some plants are poisonous to eat and can kill people or animals. Others might be toxic to touch without gloves.

2. **Get Informed:** Explore the foraging resources in your community. Organizations such as local mycological societies (groups that promote learning about wild mushrooms) or native plant societies often lead excursions into the woods that make for a fun adventure.

3. **Forage Responsibly:** Conserving wild ecosystems is key to foraging. During any kind of collection, always follow sustainability guidelines, harvest only what you need, and avoid protected areas and endangered plants.

4. **Identify and Label:** Start by looking for widespread plants that don't have toxic lookalikes, such as mulberries, black walnuts, acorns, wild blackberries, or magnolia flowers. Smartphone apps for plant identification can provide helpful guidance. Bring a magnifying glass, and keep a journal of your fascinating discoveries.

Climate Spotlight

It can be a relaxing outdoor ritual to observe the creatures who share our planet, from migrating whales to flocks of birds flying south. However, they face an increasing number of challenges due to habitat loss, which can lead to dwindling populations. Agriculture and urban development remove habitats and interrupt routes animals use to travel or migrate. Rising temperatures from global warming and waterway pollution create problems for aquatic species.

Luckily, there are solutions that can help. Combat habitat loss in your community by cultivating native plants in your backyard or community garden; the National Wildlife Federation website has lots of resources for creating a Certified Wildlife Habitat near your home or school. You can also educate yourself by learning more about the innovations at work to protect the creatures who share our planet. Get involved! It feels good to create positive change.

Bird-Friendly Buildings!

Birds don't see glass, and that's a deadly problem. An estimated one billion birds across the United States die each year when they strike windows. But new UV light–treated glass that makes windows look solid from the outside helps turn birds away from big buildings! Wondering how you can prevent birds from striking the windows of your home? Try something like stickers or window clings with patterns, which make windows look less like empty space, so they're visible to feathered friends.

Facial Recognition For Fish!

Artificial intelligence offers new ways to track endangered species that are more animal-friendly and efficient than old-fashioned methods. Some nonprofits rely on AI-powered computer vision to identify individual animals, which means they don't have to physically catch and tag animals. Endangered whale sharks used to be tracked with physical tags attached to their bodies, but now they can be tracked by their unique body markings!

Dream Destinations

Imagine swimming nearly 5,000 miles every single year. That's what humpback whales do during an annual migration that takes them from cold-water feeding grounds to warmer waters to raise calves and elude predators like orcas. Other creatures, including monarch butterflies, Arctic terns, and Atlantic salmon, also travel astoundingly long routes each year. Start your own wish list of where to see a showstopping migration in action.

Natural Bridges State Beach The Monarch Grove near this beautiful beach in Northern California draws thousands of butterflies each fall during migration. With a journey that's 2,500 or sometimes even 3,000 miles, it's no wonder they need a break! See the butterflies mid-October through February; numbers peak in November, when up to 100,000 of the winged creatures gather in the eucalyptus trees and create a dazzling sight.

Bosque del Apache National Wildlife Refuge Are you taller than a sandhill crane? Find out with a trip to this unique refuge in New Mexico to see these famously large birds—up to four feet tall with a wingspan of up to seven feet—known for their dramatic courtship dance. In addition to cranes, this swath of protected wilderness along the Rio Grande River is home to thousands of other birds in the winter, including hawks and eagles.

Cape Cod The mesmerizing spectacle of whale migration occurs off the rocky shores of Massachusetts between mid-spring and fall. Bring binoculars to spot species like humpback, minke, and finback whales. Nearby Stellwagen Bank, an 842-square-mile federally protected marine sanctuary, contributes to this being one of New England's best whale-watching destinations.

CHAPTER SIX

Our Climate

Nature brings so many things into your life: adventure, fun, beauty, mystery, and the chance to de-stress and recharge in open space. One thing you might notice, however, is that connecting with the natural world also means learning about environmental problems. Lots of these come from climate change, which affects everything on Earth—including you!

Learning about climate change is important, and if you ever feel sad, worried, or upset about what's happening, that's totally normal—it means that you care about our amazing planet. Stay in touch with your feelings, and take a break if you begin to feel overwhelmed. As we all help protect the trees, water, plants, and animals, know that even little changes can add up. And the simple act of spending more time outdoors, enjoying and learning about nature, makes a difference: That's where this book comes in, with ideas and activities that inspire you to open the door to deepen your bond with nature.

CLIMATE CHANGE: What's Happening?

Once you understand everything nature offers you, it's time to ask what you can offer the planet. That's where learning about the facts of climate change comes in. Knowing how it works will help you understand what needs to change—and inspire you to take small positive steps toward combating the problems.

IS IT REALLY GETTING HOTTER?

The most striking evidence of climate change is a rapid and widespread increase in temperature over the past century. Known as global warming, this contributes to glacier melt and rising sea levels, which destroys habitats for animals like polar bears, and threatens coastal communities.

WHY IS IT HAPPENING?

Climate change is caused by humans. Scientists have concluded that most of the warming is likely due to the burning of coal, oil, and gas (often called fossil fuels). These fuels produce major amounts of CO_2 as they burn, which, along with other **greenhouse gases**, act like a blanket or a cap, trapping heat that Earth could have otherwise radiated out into space.

WHO IS AFFECTED?

Climate change affects all of us, in part because of something called "climate disruption." The rise in global average temperatures is resulting in new, unpredictable weather patterns and conditions: for example, warming ocean waters that spawn increasingly destructive hurricanes or hotter days that create arid conditions that can lead to fast-spreading wildfires.

MAKE A MINI HABIT

SPEAK UP!

One popular saying about saving the planet from climate change goes like this: "The Earth has no voice but yours, so speak up for nature!" Do you agree it's important for people to communicate what they know about climate challenges? If so, make a goal to talk once a month with a friend or family member about environmental issues. Share what you've learned, and listen to others, and you'll be creating a community that speaks loudly and proudly on behalf of our planet.

CLIMATE CHANGE: What Can You Do?

Kids like you all over the world have worries about climate change. The best way to handle these feelings is to be proactive: create planet-friendly habits, learn about conservation, and get involved with local greening efforts.

Spread the word—and be the change you want to see in the world around you. When you take small steps to combat climate change, it adds up to create positive impact! Here are a few goals you might work toward.

* **Conserve Energy:** If you run the AC in the summer, make sure doors and windows to the outside stay tightly shut to cool air from escaping. Ditto when you open the fridge: The longer the door stays open, the more the fridge warms up and needs energy to cool down again. In winter, don't automatically turn up the heat: Put on a sweater instead!

* **Lace Up Your Sneakers:** Biking or walking just one mile a day for a year instead of taking a gas-powered car could prevent 330 pounds of CO_2 from entering the air—it would take four trees over 10 years to get rid of that much CO_2!

MAKE A MINI HABIT

BE INSPIRED

Make time to watch the famous speech given by young climate activist Greta Thunberg to world leaders at the United Nations in 2019. Learn more about her passionate advocacy for the planet by watching a documentary like *I Am Greta* or by reading one of her books about climate change.

* **Reduce and Reuse as Much as Possible:** Visit thrift stores for vintage finds and fix your stuff when it breaks instead of buying new replacements. Factories emit CO_2 when making new products.

* **Talk About It:** Communicate with your family and friends about the climate issues important to you. Talking about these issues is a great way to spread awareness *and* helps you deal with your own feelings. You can get your school involved, too: the National Wildlife Federation website has lots of information about its large network of EcoSchools, which supports environmental action through a certification program.

Getting your hands dirty with planting is fun—and good for the planet! That's especially true when it comes to native plants: These are species that have naturally evolved in a specific regions or ecosystems (rather than being introduced).

Native plants are well adapted to the conditions where they grow: A cactus that's native to the southwest can thrive in a desert environment, while a sugar maple tree needs the cooler weather of northern regions. Native plants are also key to maintaining ecological balance, since pollinators like bees and butterflies rely on them. Learn to spot the native plants in your region or even try planting some to increase biodiversity!

> # FUN FACT
>
> Butterflies' wings are clear—the colors and patterns we see are made by the reflection of the tiny scales covering them.

Monarch Butterfly Garden

Check with your local community garden or school to plant a butterfly garden that features native plants. If you have space, plant one in your own backyard, creating an important habitat for the beautiful but threatened monarch butterfly.

Activity:

1. Check out the National Wildlife Federation's program called Garden for Wildlife to learn more about what plants are native to your region and can attract monarchs.

2. Using the monarch-focused plant selections on the National Wildlife Federation website, plan your garden. You'll need "nectar plants," such as goldenrod, aster, and coneflower, and "host plants," such as milkweed, where butterflies lay their eggs.

3. Butterflies love sun! Choose a place for planting that gets at least six hours of sunlight.

4. Ask your local garden centers about the plants you've chosen. Visit a local nursery with an adult to shop for plants or order seeds online.

5. Allow your new habitat to grow, knowing your plants are providing monarch butterflies with what they need to survive and thrive.

Endangered Species Spotlight

Why exactly do wild creatures become endangered? Most of the reasons relate to human behaviors. Raise your own awareness about protecting vulnerable species—plants as well as animals—through the National Wildlife Federation. Or, find out more in person by visiting one of these fun destinations to engage with experts:

Zoos are often involved in helping endangered creatures and promoting conservation efforts. Look for specific exhibits dedicated to climate change and its effects on different species and habitats. Many accredited zoos participate in programs dedicated to saving a particular animal. For example, the San Antonio Zoo in Texas is reintroducing large numbers of captive-reared horned lizards to the wild after decades of population decline. They're working to prevent it from ever getting on the endangered species list in the first place! And in recent years, zoos around the country worked to support and protect the population of black-footed ferrets with a breeding and recovery plan that helped the creatures escape extinction.

Aquariums are far more than just a fun place to see fish! Accredited organizations run important programs that help conserve and protect marine creatures and habitats. The Monterey Bay Aquarium, in California, has helped increase the population of the endangered southern sea otter by rescuing, rehabilitating, and releasing injured and orphaned sea otters. Similarly, the Georgia Aquarium works for the preservation of endangered sea turtles and also conducts extensive research on whale sharks, tracking their migration patterns to better understand and protect these gentle giants.

Botanical Gardens are dedicated to the cultivation, study, and display of plants, and as destinations they are both fun and educational. You might walk through themed areas like a native plant garden, a tropical conservatory, or a desert plant collection. Or, learn about a specific conservation effort, such as seed banks for endangered plant species. Best of all, you'll get to spend an entire afternoon around beautiful greenery and bright flowers.

Campout Fun

In today's world, people spend a lot more time using technology like smartphones and tablets than they spend outside. The National Wildlife Federation cares deeply about helping people have positive experiences in nature. That's why the Great American Campout program was created: to provide guidelines, tips, and tricks to make camping a successful experience that you'll want to repeat again and again. Visit the website (nwf.org/great-american-campout) to find all kinds of helpful resources, and read on to learn four easy steps to enjoying your camping adventure!

1. **Choose Where to Go:** First time hitting the outdoors overnight? Don't stress. Start by researching national parks and other wilderness destinations that allow camping. Talk with a caring adult about booking campsites in advance through places like Reserve America.

2. **Plan Ahead:** Will you hike? Kayak? Spend lazy days by the creek? Check out what adventure activities will be available where you want to camp, and plan accordingly. Find where to rent gear before departing: It might be easier to rent kayaks and life jackets on site, for example, than to transport them from elsewhere yourself.

3. **Pack It Up:** Once you've picked your place, it's time to figure out what you'll need to take with you. Download a camping checklist from the NWF website for a list of essential items.

4. **Leave No Trace:** No matter where you camp, respect the environment you are entering and leave it better than you found it. Reduce your impact by hiking and camping only in the marked areas and staying on established trails. Maintain fire safety at all times, and pick up your own trash and any other trash you find. "Leave no trace" is not just a list of rules—it's an attitude!

Make a "Green Hour" Goal

When was the last time you spent an hour outside? The truth is that screens occupy a lot of time: The average American kid spends more than seven hours each day in front of a screen!

What if instead of being part of that trend, you carved out 60 minutes of your day to spend in nature? Commit to trying it every day for one week, to start—and see how it goes. Think of it as your "green hour" and spend the time trying the activities in this book or simply enjoying the fresh air.

MAKE A MINI HABIT

SAY NO TO STRAWS

Refusing a plastic straw can save a marine animal's life and decrease pollution from single-use plastic. Straws can harm and kill seabirds, fish, sea turtles, manatees, dolphins, and other animals. Ask for drinks without straws at restaurants and coffee shops. Shift to using paper straws that are biodegradable or reusable metal straws that can be cleaned regularly.

Make an Eco-Friendly Earth Flag

Try your hand at making a flag to signify your commitment to nature! Use upcycled materials and your own artistry for this easy activity inspired by the view of planet Earth from space.

What You'll Need:

Paper

Pencils or crayon

Paint

Old T-shirt, pillowcase, or other fabric

Glue

Scissors

Activity:

1. Create a flag design inspired by our round blue planet. You might choose blue and green stripes to represent the oceans and forests or paint a circle of swirling colors.

2. Find your fabric: Look for lightweight colored fabrics or white if you want to paint it (use paper if you don't have fabric).

3. Cut your main piece of fabric to size. Or, cut strips of fabric to the length you want and glue their edges together. Decorate your flag with paint or glued pieces of colored fabric.

4. Find a long sturdy item you can use as a handle or "flagpole," like a fallen tree branch or an old broom handle.

5. Once your design is finished and dried, wrap the edge of the fabric around the handle, and glue it into place. After the glue sets, unfurl your flag and fly it high!

Climate Spotlight

People do so many things in a day that demand energy: cook in the kitchen, use a computer, charge a smartphone, or drive in the car. That all comes from one of two types of energy: renewable sources, like wind and water; or nonrenewable sources, like fossil fuels such as coal, oil, and natural gas. You might have noticed examples of renewable energy in your own region, like windmills or solar panels on buildings. There are lots of advancing technologies at work to make renewable energy more widespread.

Sun-Powered Buildings! You might not think of buildings as being smart—but they can be! One new technology that can make structures more energy "smart" is something called building-integrated photovoltaics (BIPV). That's a fancy way to say they have solar panels integrated right into windows, roofs, or the front walls of buildings to create clean energy and reduce carbon emissions.

Offshore Wind Farms! Have you ever flown a kite or had an umbrella snatched away at the beach, because it was so windy? The prevalence of high winds is one reason why massive windmills are being built out in the ocean. South Fork Wind, about 30 miles off the coast of New York City, is a wind farm with colossal steel turbines. It generates 132 megawatts of offshore wind energy to power more than 70,000 homes. Producing energy this way reduces pollution, thanks to the natural, never-ending resource that is wind.

SCIENCE SAYS

How Does Water Turn Into Electricity?

Flowing water becomes electricity with the help of a hydropower plant. How does it work? When water flows through a dam, it spins turbines connected to generators. The mechanical energy from the turbines is transformed into electrical energy, which is then transmitted through power lines. This renewable and clean source of power relies on a natural resource and doesn't release planet-warming emissions like fossil fuels do.

Dream Destinations

Have you ever heard of a conservation vacation? It's a trip that's fun and adventurous but also lets you check out an important conservation effort. You might return home committed to new habits that help protect the planet and its animals. Depending on where you live, you might even be able to take a "conservation vacation" day trip by visiting a marine mammal center, land conservancy, park, or nature preserve near you. Start your own wish list of destinations where you can see amazing conservation efforts! Here are a couple ideas to get you started:

Visit the Sea Turtles of Padre Island Padre Island National Seashore in Texas is home to multiple types of sea turtles that are endangered or threatened, like loggerhead, and hawksbill turtles. The area also holds the largest nesting ground of Kemp's ridley sea turtles in the United States. You can even attend public hatching events where baby sea turtles make their way to the Gulf.

Go Where the Bison Roam Learn more about the near extinction and recovery of these remarkable animals with a visit to Yellowstone National Park in Montana. The park is the only place in the United States where bison have lived continuously since prehistoric times. This successfully restored population was on the brink of extinction just over a century ago.

MORE RESOURCES

APPS (FOR KIDS AGES 8+)

Nature Activity Apps:

Merlin Bird ID: Identifies birds based on real-time sounds you record

Pl@ntNet: Identifies plants based on photographs you supply

Seek by iNaturalist: Identifies types of birds, amphibians, plants, and fungi using photographs you supply

Star Chart: GPS to explore the skies, like a virtual planetarium

Emotional Well-Being Apps:

Calm: Meditation and relaxation techniques for kids

Three Good Things: Teen-created journaling app for kids

BOOKS

A Girl's Guide to the Wild: Be an Adventure-Seeking Outdoor Explorer! by Ruby McConnell (Little Bigfoot, 2019)

All the Feelings Under the Sun: How to Deal With Climate Change by Leslie Davenport (Magination Press, 2021)

How to Change Everything: The Young Human's Guide to Protecting the Planet and Each Other by Naomi Klein with Rebecca Stefoff (Atheneum Books for Young Readers, 2022)

WEBSITES

America's State Parks: americasstateparks.org

Common Sense Media (for age-based ratings for nature documentaries and movies): commonsensemedia.org

Gloria Barron Prize for Young Heroes (profiles of young leaders ages 8 to 18 making a positive difference for people and the environment): barronprize.org

NASA: nasa.gov or spaceplace.nasa. gov

National Geographic Kids: kids. nationalgeographic.com

National Park Service: nps.gov or nps.gov/kids

National Wildlife Federation: nwf. org

Ranger Rick: rangerrick.org

Ultimate Camp Resource: ultimatecampresource.com

World Wildlife Fund: worldwildlife.org

GLOSSARY

biodegradable—when something can be broken down by living things such as bacteria

carbon dioxide (CO$_2$)—a colorless gas produced by respiration and the burning and breaking down of organic substances and fossil fuels; absorbed by plants during photosynthesis

carbon footprint—the amount of greenhouse gases given off by a person's activities or a product's manufacture; to measure environmental impact

climate change—the change in global climate patterns linked to increased emissions of carbon dioxide and other greenhouse gases from human activity

compass rose– A circle found on a map that shows the directions north, south, east, and west labeled.

conservation—the preservation and protection of something (such as the environment) by keeping it from mistreatment or damage

extinct—when something no longer exists, especially a plant or animal species

foliage—the leaves of a plant or multiple plants

forest bathing—the practice of spending intentional calm and quiet time among trees for nature observation and relaxation; known in Japan as shinrin yoku

geyser—a hot spring that repeatedly erupts in jets of water and steam

global warming—the increase in the average temperature of Earth's atmosphere and oceans; connected to increased greenhouse gas emissions caused by human activity

gorge—a narrow opening between hills or rocky walls

greenhouse gas—gases like carbon dioxide or methane that absorb and trap heat in Earth's atmosphere, contributing to global warming

invasive species—a plant or animal that is introduced to a different ecosystem than where it is naturally found and whose presence causes environmental harm

mindfulness—the state of being aware and paying attention to the present moment, without judgment

nocturnal—relating to or occurring at night

observe—to watch carefully or take notice of

organism—a living thing that functions as a whole yet has many related parts, such as a plant or an animal

pollution—a state of contamination resulting from substances being added to the environment at harmful levels

reclaim—to reuse materials or structures that have been used before to achieve a different and desirable state

recycle—to process and convert waste such as glass, cans, or cardboard into new materials that can be used again

reflection—the bouncing back of light or sound waves from a surface

reforestation—the regeneration of trees after forest loss through natural seeding or intentional planting

resilience—the ability to adapt or recover quickly from adversity or misfortune

restorative—something that helps renew feelings of strength, health, or well-being

rhodopsin—a light-sensitive receptor protein in the rod cells of the eye's retina; important to vision in dim light

species—a group of genetically similar organisms that have the ability to interbreed and produce fertile offspring

sustainable—using or harvesting a natural resource in a way that ensures the resource is not depleted and the environment is not permanently damaged

tree line—the level on a mountain above which there is no tree growth

urban—of and relating to the city, areas where many people live and work, resulting in dense development

INDEX

PHOTO CREDITS

ABOUT THE AUTHOR

Kate Chynoweth is the author of a half dozen nonfiction books, and her writing on health and wellness appears in various publications. She lives in Northern California with her family.

ABOUT MAGINATION PRESS

The American Psychological Association works to advance psychology as a science and profession, as a means to improve health and human welfare. APA publishes books for young readers under its imprint, Magination Press. It's the combined power of psychology and literature that helps kids navigate life's challenges a little more easily. Visit maginationpress.org and @MaginationPress on Facebook, X, Instagram, and Pinterest.

ABOUT NWF

The National Wildlife Federation, America's largest and most trusted conservation organization, works across the country to unite Americans from all walks of life in giving wildlife a voice. NWF has been on the front lines for wildlife since 1936, fighting for the conservation values that are woven into the fabric of our nation's collective heritage. NWF is also a publisher of magazines for children. For over 55 years, *Ranger Rick Magazine* has aimed to inspire in its readers a greater understanding of the natural world, a deep love of nature and wildlife, and a lasting commitment to conservation and environmental action.